# The Shadow Man

by
Anne Schraff

Perfection Learning
Logan, Iowa 51546

Cover: Doug Knutson

**1** DAMIEN STARED OUT the window. The black sedan was still there, parked right across the street. Damien had noticed it earlier, just before he'd gone to the kitchen to eat breakfast.

Now the morning sunlight was reflecting brightly off the car's smooth surfaces. The glare made Damien squint. It took a moment before he realized that the driver was staring right at the window where Damien stood.

"Mama, come here!" Damien called. "There's a strange guy outside looking us over."

Damien's mother hurried over to the window, but she was too late. The black sedan screeched away from the curb before she could catch a good look at it.

Damien turned toward his mother. He noticed a worried look in her eye.

"Hey, what's the matter, Mama?" asked Damien. "Is somebody after us or what?"

"Don't be silly, Damien," his mother said. "Who would want to bother us?"

Damien knew she was right. Why would anyone make trouble for a third-grade teacher and her fifteen-year-old son? Damien felt a little guilty for giving her a scare.

"Hey, I've got it, Mama," said Damien with a grin. "Maybe he's like our guardian angel or something. Or maybe he came to give us a million bucks. Too bad I scared him off, huh?"

"Yeah, too bad, Damien," said his mother with a laugh. But it was a shallow laugh. Damien could tell she was actually worried about the watcher.

His mother stared out the window for a few seconds. Then she turned to Damien. "Uh, honey, what did that man in the car look like?" she asked.

"I didn't get a real good look. He was a black guy in his thirties, I guess. Kind of light-skinned. He was driving a pretty cool car."

Damien's mother took a sip of her coffee and Damien noticed her hand shook. That just wasn't like her. She was one strong lady, cool in times of trouble. Ever since his father had been killed, his mother had calmly dealt with all the family problems. He'd rarely seen her so uneasy.

"Mama, do you know something about this guy?" he asked.

"Of course not," she said. "I'm just curious." She laughed uneasily again. "I'll bet he wasn't even looking at our place. You probably imagined it. That's just like you, Damien. You watch too many cop shows."

Damien didn't argue. But he was sure the man had looked squarely at him. And almost as soon as their eyes met, the car had shot off like a rocket. Damien wished he'd gotten a better look. But there was nothing he could do about it now. He finished his orange juice and slung his book bag over his shoulder.

"Gotta go, Mama," he said.

"Yeah, me too," she said with a nervous smile. She quickly swallowed the rest of her coffee.

Damien watched her from the corner of his eye. His mother was small and slim.

She had a nice smile and lively, long-lashed eyes. Her skin was a deep cocoa color, much richer than Damien's.

Damien was often struck by how beautiful his mother was. But right now, he was worried about her. He felt sure she was afraid of something.

"Mama, is anything wrong?" he asked.

"No. Why?"

"I dunno. Just a hunch."

His mother smiled that big warm smile of hers. She seemed to relax a bit. "I'm not sure which will make you poorer the quicker: following your hunches or burning your money," she said.

"Yeah. I guess. But listen, you can talk to me about anything. You know that, don't you?" Then with a grin he added, "I'm the man of the house, you know."

Damien's mother laughed sweetly. "Yeah, that's right," she said. "But you're also a Wilson High student who's got to get to class on time."

On his way to the door, Damien glanced at the pictures on the wall. One was of his mother from her college days.

She stood holding a clarinet and grinning at the camera. "Jessie Cole, jazz fan," it read. Damien's dad had loved that picture and insisted it hang where he could see it.

The other photo was even older. It had hung there for as long as Damien could remember. Even so, he hardly ever walked by it without stopping to look at it.

The picture was from Charles Blair's high school senior yearbook. It was one of the best pictures anybody had taken of him. He was twenty-six when he died, but he was only eighteen when that picture was taken.

It always made Damien feel strange to look at that handsome high school boy. Damien's friends had fathers who were mature men. But in Damien's mind, his father was a kid who'd never grow older. How could you think of somebody that young as your father?

The man in the picture wore a confident smile. He looked as if he had the future all planned out like a route on a road map. He never foresaw the terrible end to his life.

Damien thought back to when he was a kid. It had been really hard for him to understand what had happened to his father. He used to ask his mother the same questions again and again.

"How did he die?" Damien would ask her. "Who killed him?"

He remembered how his mother would take him onto her lap. Then gently and patiently, she'd tell him the whole story as if for the first time.

"He was walking home from the store with a carton of milk," she would say. "I saw him out the window. Suddenly a car came out of nowhere and hit him. I watched him fall. I remember the milk hitting the pavement. It splashed up like a fountain.

"Then the car sped away. It all happened so fast, I didn't get a good look at the driver or the car. Nobody else did either.

"So nobody knows, Damien. Nobody knows who killed him. And now it's old and finished business. We've got to get on with our lives."

Her words echoed through Damien's head as he stood gazing at the picture. He had long since quit asking his mother about his father's death. There was probably nothing else she could add to the story. But his mind was still full of the same old questions.

If only you could tell me, Damien thought as he stared at the picture.

Then his mother's voice jolted him from his thoughts.

"Damien, come out of the clouds!" she said. "Hurry now, or you'll be late!"

"Okay, Mama. I'm going," Damien called.

He flew out the door and down the steps. By the time he hit the sidewalk, he was running. He didn't want to be late.

Unlike so many of his classmates, Damien actually liked school. He even enjoyed things the other kids hated. For instance, in English class they were reading *A Tale of Two Cities* by Charles Dickens. Everyone else was complaining about how hard it was. Damien, on the other hand, couldn't put it down.

Not that everything about school was great. Damien was reminded of that fact when he got to school. There, standing squarely in the doorway, waited Brad Stanton.

Brad was a big kid, a good six inches taller than Damien. He was sixteen, but he was in Damien's class because he'd flunked a year.

As Damien tried to get through the door, Brad leaned back. He stretched out a leg, blocking Damien's way.

"What's your hurry?" sneered Brad.

"Get out of my way," said Damien.

" 'Fraid you'll be late for class? You're such a pathetic case. You know that, little man?"

"Don't call me that."

"Little man? Like I said—pathetic."

"Cool it, Stanton. At least I'll grow up someday. Can't say the same for you."

Brad squinted menacingly and stepped forward. He shoved Damien back with his fist. "You making fun of me?"

Damien was scared, but only a little. Brad always talked tough. Yet Damien knew he was a coward deep down. A group of kids started to form around them, watching eagerly. Damien wished they'd mind their own business.

"Let me through," said Damien.

"Oh, no. Not yet. I got an assignment for you to do first."

"Assignment?"

"Yeah, little man. Know that paper old man Hall wants us to write? The one about that stupid book we've been reading?"

"Yeah. So what?"

"So you're gonna write mine for me."

Damien shook his head. "I can't do that, Stanton."

"Why not?"

"I just can't."

"Ohhh, I get it," Brad crowed. "That would be *cheating*. And it's not nice to cheat, huh?"

"Something like that, yeah."

"Well, well. Just imagine a Blair trying to preach to me," Brad sneered.

"Everybody knows your old man got blown away for cheating somebody on a drug deal."

Fury flooded Damien. He lunged at Brad, knocking the older boy off his feet. Then Damien straddled him and grabbed a handful of Brad's shirt. The air was filled with the voices of other kids, cheering and goading him on.

"Liar!" Damien screamed in Brad's face. "You take that back or I'll smash your face!"

"Let me up," Brad pleaded. "Okay, okay, I'm lying!"

Damien backed off. "Don't you ever say anything like that again," he muttered.

Damien saw hatred boiling over in Brad's eyes. He knew just what Brad was thinking. Brad hated being beaten, especially by a younger kid. But what he hated most was that other kids had seen it. Pretty soon it would be all over school.

Brad got to his feet and shot one last burning look at Damien. *I'll pay you back,* his eyes were saying.

As Damien picked up his book bag, he noticed two faces in the crowd: James Moran and Tara Kimbo, his best friends. Damien walked over to them, eager to escape the crowd.

"Hey, you really made your point, Damien," James said to him. "You got a great career ahead of you in All-Star Wrestling!"

Tara frowned. "Yeah, Damien. Very classy," she said. "I guess I gave you too much credit. You're just what this school needs—another macho punk."

Ashamed, Damien lowered his eyes and walked off. He felt stupid for getting into the fight in the first place. Why had he let that loudmouth Stanton set him off?

After all, he hadn't even said anything new to Damien. That gossip about his father being mixed up with drugs had started the day Charles Blair died. Some of the neighbors said that's why he died—over a deal that had gone sour. They said he was just another young man who'd been killed because he played with fire.

But Damien's mother always swore that wasn't how it was at all. Damien remembered one conversation in particular. He'd come home in tears after some kids taunted him about his father.

His mother had dried his eyes and then sat down with him. "Folks around here see too much crime. They think everybody is crooked, honey," she explained to Damien.

"But no matter what stupid gossip you hear about your father, don't you believe a word of it. Your father never touched drugs. Not to use and not to sell."

His mother shook her head. "Oh, he had his chances. He could have made a pile of money that way. But he never did. He earned his pay at the gas station and went to school nights to be an engineer. He was just about ready to graduate. But then that hit-and-run driver came around the corner and killed him."

Tears came to his mother's eyes. But her voice remained soft and steady. "It was an accident. A stupid, rotten accident. The person who did it ran. Probably wasn't even a bad person. Just a coward."

Damien stood outside the school, remembering his mother's words. He believed her. How could he help but believe her? She'd never lie about something so important.

But still, there were those rumors. Why did people say things like that? How did the rumors start?

It bothered Damien to even think about such questions. Besides, it was time to get to class.

Damien checked in his bag for his English paper. Then something caught his eye.

Damien slowly raised his head and stared. Sitting across the street was a black sedan. The same black sedan he'd seen earlier. And the same man sat behind the wheel—looking straight at Damien.

He followed me to school, Damien thought. A chill went up his spine. The man was really starting to scare him.

But scared as he was, he couldn't just stand by and do nothing. He had to find out once and for all what this was about.

Damien started across the street toward the car.

**2** DAMIEN NEARED THE car. His eyes locked with the stranger's. This time, he was close enough to notice something strange about the man's eyes. What was it, exactly?

Before Damien could get a really good look, the man started the car. Then with a burst of speed, he drove away.

Damien's hands swung in frustration at his sides. What was this guy trying to do? What did he want? And what was it about his eyes that seemed so strange?

The questions buzzed like hornets in Damien's brain. Damien wished he'd been clearheaded enough to look at the license plate number. But what good would that have done? What was he going to do— report this guy to the police? The man hadn't done anything illegal. At least, not so far.

Damien headed back to school and met James at the door. "What was that all about?" James asked.

"That guy in the black car," said Damien. "Did you see him?"

James shrugged. "Just some guy looking for action."

"Ever see him before, James?"

"Nah. Why? How come you're so interested?"

"Because he was in front of our apartment this morning. He was just staring up at our window. When he saw me looking, he was out of there fast. And just now he was watching me from his car. When he saw me coming toward him, he took off again. What's he after me for?"

James laughed. "Maybe he's from some gym where they want fresh young fists. In this corner, Rockin' Damien Blair!"

"I'm serious, man," Damien said irritably as they walked toward class. "You can joke about it, but I don't like him hanging around. My mama's scared. She tried to hide it, but I could tell."

"What's there to be scared of?" James asked. "You sure don't have enough money for a thief to be staking out your place. And you and your mama aren't doing anything illegal. So there's no reason for some plainclothes cop to be spying on you, is there?''

"Guess not," said Damien.

Still, Damien felt uncertain. He knew that he and his mama had never done anything wrong. But what about all that gossip about his father? Damien had even heard rumors that his dad had made a bunch of money and stashed it somewhere. What if the guy in the car believed those rumors? What if he thought Damien and his mother were hoarding a pile of drug money?

Then a thought came to Damien that he'd always hurriedly rejected before. Was he absolutely sure all that stuff about his father was false? Or could his dad have even lied to his mama? Had his dad been hiding some terrible secrets all along?

Damien hated the man in the car for putting such awful ideas in his head. And he was glad English class was coming up. Maybe it would get his mind off this whole thing.

The bell rang and Damien and his

classmates slid into their seats. Mr. Hall, their teacher, was a short, chunky man. He wore little round-rimmed glasses that made him look like an owl.

Mr. Hall leaned back against his desk. "Well, we're most of the way through *A Tale of Two Cities,*" he said. "So what do you think of it so far? What do you like or dislike about it?"

"I liked that big old head chopper," said one kid in the back. "That's sure one way to cure a headache!"

Some of the others laughed. Mr. Hall shook his head and smiled patiently.

"You mean the guillotine," said Mr. Hall. "I wonder, Sam, if you'd find it so amusing if you actually saw one of those executions. You know, the guillotine got its name from its inventor, Dr. Joseph Guillotin. He'd intended it as a painless form of execution. But was it really so painless? None of its victims ever said.

"Imagine how it must have felt to die that way. Even if the actual moment of death was painless, everything up to that point was terrifying. You'd be driven

through the streets in a little cart. A tumbril, it was called. An angry mob sur-
rounded you on all sides, jeering and
shouting. Then came the climb up the
stairs to the platform where the guillotine
stood. Its huge blade was covered with
the blood of those who'd already died that
day. You could see the waiting wagons
full of headless bodies. And you'd realize
that the same fate awaited you."

Damien leaned forward as Mr. Hall
talked. The teacher's voice rolled on
dramatically like a marvelous train. He
made you feel like you were right there
in the Reign of Terror.

"Let's hear some other comments,"
said Mr. Hall.

Damien raised his hand. "The book
really shows how the French Revolution
went wrong, doesn't it?" he said. "I
mean, the whole idea at the beginning
was to make France more just and fair for
everybody. The Reign of Terror was only supposed to get rid of selfish
aristocrats and enemies of France. But it
didn't work out that way."

"It certainly didn't," said Mr. Hall. "Thousands of people died. Some were guilty, but others were innocent. And many of those who rebelled became just as brutal as those they fought against."

Mr. Hall's bright, dark eyes searched his students' faces. "What does that tell you about human nature?"

"That violence doesn't work," said Damien. He couldn't help thinking again about his stupid fight with Brad Stanton.

"It's like in this neighborhood," added Tara. "A couple of gangs start fighting over turf. Then some little kid gets blown away just because he happened to be in the wrong place."

Was that what happened to my father? Damien wondered. Was he just an innocent victim?

After class, Damien walked up to Mr. Hall's desk. Sometimes he stayed to talk with Mr. Hall if they both had a free period.

"I still haven't finished the book but I want to ask you something," Damien said. "It's about Sydney Carton."

"Oh, yes," said Mr. Hall, leaning back in his chair and smiling. "Sydney Carton is one of Dickens' most fascinating characters."

"Yeah, but he kind of bothers me," continued Damien. "At the beginning of the book, he's just this drunk who only thinks about himself. But then towards the end, he switches places with a man who's supposed to be executed. Suddenly he's willing to give up his life for this other man."

Mr. Hall nodded. "Pretty noble stuff."

"I guess. Actually, it seems pretty strange to me."

"Why?"

"I just have trouble believing it."

"So you don't think people can change their ways?"

Damien thought about Brad Stanton. He couldn't imagine Brad ever coming to somebody's rescue. And Brad sure wouldn't die for the sake of a friend—if he had one. Then again, Damien had trouble imagining doing such a thing *himself.*

Finally he said, "I haven't seen it happen too much," said Damien. "I mean people changing for the better. Do you really think a lot of people would do what Sydney Carton did?'' he asked Mr. Hall.

"I'm not sure I can answer that question," said Mr. Hall. "It's something you have to learn for yourself. Different people see life in different ways. It's all a matter of experience."

Damien found himself thinking again about his father. Was he a hero or a crook? Maybe Mr. Hall could tell him.

Damien hesitated. "Did you know my dad, Charles Blair?" he asked.

"Yes, I did, Damien," said Mr. Hall.

"You remember that he was killed by a hit-and-run driver," Damien said.

"Yes. It was a terrible thing."

"Well, I was just a little kid when he died. I really didn't know him. I wondered if you could tell me what kind of a guy he was."

Mr. Hall folded his small, dark brown hands together and rested them on his desk. "Is there a reason this is troubling you now, Damien?" he asked gently.

"Yeah, sort of. I keep hearing rumors.

Like people saying my dad was mixed up in drugs. They claim that's why he was killed."

Mr. Hall sighed. "Damien, I've been teaching here at Wilson High for twenty-seven years. Some of the kids in my classes now are the children of my older students from way back when. Over twenty years ago, your father was in my English class. Charles was a fine boy. Not as bright as you are, Damien, but smart enough. And he *never* caused any serious trouble in my class—or in this school—that I ever heard about."

Mr. Hall paused thoughtfully. "You just asked me about Sydney Carton," he said. "You wondered if people ever really do noble, self-sacrificing things. Well, I think some people do. And I believe your father was one of them. I can't think of anything he wouldn't have done for friends or family."

Damien felt his throat tighten with emotion. His eyes burned a little. "Thanks, Mr. Hall," he said. "That's really nice to know."

Damien turned to go out the door. Then Mr. Hall said, "Thank *you,* Damien."

"For what?"

"Well, for liking *A Tale of Two Cities,* I guess. For actually thinking about what you've read. It makes my job seem a little more worthwhile."

Damien smiled. He wanted to tell Mr. Hall how much he liked class. But he was afraid it would come out sounding stupid. Besides, Mr. Hall probably already knew.

"Have a nice weekend, Mr. Hall," said Damien. Then he left.

The rest of the day dragged on. Damien couldn't help but worry about the man in the black car. That made the classes pass slowly.

At the end of the school day, Damien ran into Tara in the hall. She noticed his worried expression and asked him what was the matter.

Damien was glad she asked. He liked Tara. In fact, they'd even gone out on a few casual dates. She wasn't like a lot of the other girls who tried to act like rock music queens. She wasn't stuck-up or weird. She was just nice and natural—you could talk to her about anything. And she had more common sense than any other kid he knew.

Damien figured that maybe Tara could give him some good advice. So he told her about the man in the car.

"Why don't you call the cops?" she asked.

"Well, he hasn't really done anything yet."

"What do you mean he hasn't done anything? He's *following* you, isn't he? How many times have you seen him?"

"Just twice, so far. This morning outside our apartment. Then I spotted him a while later across from the school."

Tara laughed softly. "Just *twice?* Damien, are you sure this guy is really following you? I mean, couldn't it be just a coincidence?"

"You didn't see the expression on his face. He was staring right at me. And he looks kind of strange, Tara. He dresses okay and he drives a good car. But he still

sort of looks like a bum. And there's
something about his eyes . . . ''

Damien's voice trailed off. He shook
his head. ''I'm sounding crazy, right?''

Tara touched his arm reassuringly.
''No, Damien. No, you're not. Around this
neighborhood, you get scared sometimes,
that's all. Everybody does. You'd be
dumb if you didn't. There've been lots of
times when I thought I was being
followed. I look over my shoulder all the
time. But you can't get carried away with
crazy ideas.''

As they neared Damien's locker, they
noticed a small group of kids around it.
James stood in the middle of them. He
was reading a note attached to the locker.

''Hey, Damien, you'd better take a look
at this,'' said James. He handed Damien
the note.

*I'll send flowers when you die, sucker,*
it read.

''Somebody's idea of a joke, I guess,''
said Damien.

''Yeah, a real Stanton-type joke,'' said
James. ''It's typed so you won't recognize

the handwriting. What a coward, huh? Hey! There he is now!" Before Damien could stop him, James called out, "Real tough, Stanton!"

Brad whirled and came back towards James. "What're you talking about?" he growled.

"Never mind," said Damien.

"You trying to start something again, Blair?" Brad asked.

"Quit pretending," James said. He snatched the note out of Damien's hand and gave it to Brad.

Brad read it and laughed. "Looks like somebody really hates your guts, huh, Damien? Well, if you're trying to nail whoever wrote it, lots of luck. Way I figure, it could be just about anybody in this school!"

Damien's temper flared. "I know who wrote it, Stanton," he shot back.

"Hey, you saying *I* wrote it? This is kid's stuff, Blair. When I go after you, you won't even see it coming."

Brad swaggered away.

"He wrote it, all right," said James.

"He's just stupid enough to pull a stunt like that."

"It doesn't matter," said Damien. He crushed the note and threw it in the trash. "I've got too much other stuff on my mind to worry about this."

Damien strode out of the school. When he reached the sidewalk, he quickly scanned the street. He half expected to see the black sedan parked there. But it was nowhere in sight.

Damien smiled with relief. Maybe Tara was right after all. He'd just let his imagination get away from him. He'd probably never see the guy again.

But as Damien started walking home, he got a spooky feeling. It was as though someone was watching him.

Damien tried to ignore the feeling for a while. He fought the impulse to turn and look. He reminded himself again of what Tara had said.

But after a minute, he couldn't stand it anymore. He wheeled around and looked.

Damien felt his heart slam against his

ribs. The black car was cruising near the curb just a few yards behind him.

**3** DAMIEN STOOD FROZEN in his tracks as the car passed by. For a brief moment, he stared into the car window. He tried to glimpse the man's face. But the buildings on either side of the street blocked the sun, cloaking the driver in shadow. Then in another instant, the car turned the corner and was gone.

Damien couldn't move for a few seconds. Then he took a deep, shaky breath and slowly started walking again. But he couldn't help looking over his shoulder from time to time.

Damien felt a little safer when he reached King Avenue. Here little grocery stores, secondhand clothing and furniture shops, a cafe, a laundromat, and liquor stores lined the street. Some of the businesses were run-down. Still, the place was full of people and life.

Damien wasn't so sure what he thought about the graffiti that peppered the building walls. Some of it told stories of hate and love. Some of it just said that somebody had been there and wanted to be remembered.

Not all the graffiti was ugly. A few designs were even artistic. But Damien always thought there was something sad about the scrawls. To him, they seemed to silently shout, "Look at me! I exist! I'm here! Why can't you see me, man?"

As if in answer, a police car drove by. The cop driving the car waved and nodded at Damien. The police in this neighborhood usually tried to be nice to kids. They hoped a friendly attitude would encourage kids to stay out of trouble.

Damien wondered if he should stop this cop and tell him about the black car. But before he could decide, the police car turned a corner.

Oh well, Damien thought. I'm pretty safe here. He gave a casual glance back to prove it to himself and nearly cried out in surprise.

It couldn't be! The man was there again. But this time he was on foot, walking close behind Damien! He was wearing a long, dark overcoat over his sweater. But Damien was sure it was the same man.

Damien stopped and braced himself.
This had to stop. He wasn't going to let
this guy keep chasing him.

But before Damien could get a word
out, the man called to him. "Hey, kid,"
he said. "You dropped something."

The man held out a fat envelope.

"I didn't drop that," Damien protested.

The man still held it out to Damien.
"Look, kid. It's full of money. You don't
want to lose something like that."

Damien stared as the man loosened the
flap on the envelope. A thick stack of bills
peeked out.

Damien could scarcely believe his eyes.
He'd never seen that much cash except
on a TV show.

Yet Damien didn't let the money daz-
zle him. At any second this guy might
grab him and force him into a car or
something. Suddenly the streets didn't
seem nearly as crowded as they had a moment before.

"That's not mine," Damien stammered

out.

The man fingered the contents of the envelope. "About two hundred in here, looks like," he said. He stepped closer and Damien moved back cautiously.

"Look, I'm sure I saw it drop from your school bag," the man said. He was close enough now for Damien to get a good look at his face. He noticed that though the man wasn't old, his face looked tired and saggy.

And now Damien realized what was strange about the man's eyes. They were dark blue. Damien had never seen a black man with blue eyes.

"I said it's not mine," Damien insisted.

"Take it," said the man. "I bet you could use it."

"What am I supposed to do for it?" Damien demanded. When somebody gave you that kind of cash around here, you could bet it was to do something illegal. A lot of kids got started selling drugs that way.

"Nothing," said the man with a hint of weariness in his voice. "It's found money. Just take it. I'm sure your mother needs it."

Damien was surprised at how soft and kind the man's voice was. Somehow, he wanted to trust that voice. But he couldn't.

Damien stared at the man for a minute. Then he said, "I saw you this morning watching our apartment. I saw you at school too. Who are you?"

The man sighed tiredly. He shrugged and said, "Just take the money and give it to your mother. Okay?" He held out the envelope again with the tempting bills.

Damien knew how his mama scrimped and saved. She'd clip coupons to shave twenty cents off an item here and there. Two hundred dollars would look like a fortune to her. But something was very, very wrong here.

"What's your name?" Damien asked.

"Willis Tate," answered the man.

"Well, you'd better leave us alone, Mr. Tate," said Damien. "I'll call the cops if you don't."

Damien stood there, waiting for the

man to turn and go. But Willis Tate didn't move. He just stood there, looking at Damien sadly.

Finally Damien turned and walked away. He longed to run. But he wasn't going to let this guy know he was scared.

When he reached his building, Damien rushed up the stairs and unlocked the door. He knew his mother would still be at a faculty meeting at her school. So Damien would be alone in the apartment. He didn't usually mind that, but today was different. Today he wished his mother were home right now.

Though the sun shone brightly, Damien turned on all the lights in the apartment. Cautiously he peered out the window to see if anybody was parked across the street. He was relieved to see there wasn't any black car there.

Damien started on his homework. He did his math problems. Then he started to read the last chapter of *A Tale of Two Cities*. Sydney Carton was riding the tumbril to the guillotine. Despite the fact that he was going to his death, Carton took time to comfort a girl who was also supposed to be executed.

Damien was so fascinated by the scene that he forgot for a moment about Willis Tate. He turned the pages, anxious to get to the end. Was Dickens really going to let his hero die?

Damien flipped to the last page. Then he heard it. Footsteps on the stairs leading to the apartment.

Damien snapped the book shut and listened fearfully. He had locked and double-locked the door. Even so, the footsteps on the stairs turned him numb.

Aside from Damien and his mother, the only person to use those stairs was old Mrs. Osborne from next door. But this didn't sound like her footfall. A stranger was coming up the steps, getting ever nearer to the door. From the sound of the steps, it was someone big and young— like the shadow man who had been following him.

Damien stared at the door. What if the man threw himself against it? Would the old wood splinter and shatter as it did in the movies? Would Damien soon see a hand coming through a jagged hole to unlock the chain?

Then what would Damien do? Run to his bedroom? No, the bedroom door didn't have a lock on it. Jump out the window? It was three stories to the street below.

The footsteps drew closer. The stalker had reached the last landing and was still approaching. Now he was in the hall just outside the door. The footsteps stopped.

Damien pressed himself back against the wall and stared at the door. Then he remembered the telephone. The police! Damien bounded across the room and grabbed the phone, ready to call.

Then something began to slide under the door. It was an envelope—the same one the man had offered Damien a little while ago. It was still fat with money and had to be forced under the door. Like a fat worm, it inched slowly forward.

When the envelope was all the way inside, Damien heard the footsteps again. But this time they were going away.

Down, down to the front door they echoed. Then the door opened and closed. Finally there was only the sound of his own heart pounding.

Damien ran to the window and looked outside, but he couldn't see the man. Was he still out there somewhere? Was he standing in a nearby doorway out of sight?

Still nervous, Damien turned and looked at the envelope. Cautiously he walked over and picked it up. The money was still inside. But this time, there was a handwritten note wrapped around it.

*Please accept this money* was all the note said.

Damien sat down at the kitchen table and stared at the message. He read it over and over again, wondering what to do.

Damien was still sitting at the table when he heard footsteps on the stairs again. Immediately he tensed up.

But as the steps neared, Damien relaxed. This time he knew it was his mother. She always ran up the stairs, just like a young girl.

His mother came through the door and set her school bag on the floor. "Hi, Damien. How was your day?" she asked.

Without a word, Damien handed her the envelope. His mother examined the note and the money. Then she looked at Damien curiously.

"What's this all about?" she asked.

"It's from the guy who was watching us this morning," said Damien. "He tried to give it to me on the street. I wouldn't take it. I thought maybe he was trying to get me to do something illegal. But then he came here and pushed the money under the door."

Damien's mother sat down in an overstuffed chair with the envelope in her hand. She studied its contents with a worried expression.

"Did the man say what his name was?" she asked.

"Yeah," said Damien. "Willis Tate."

His mother nodded sadly, as if she'd been expecting to hear the name. Then she got up and went to the bread drawer.

There was a little strongbox there. Damien's mother hid some cash and important papers in it. She hoped a burglar wouldn't look there right away. Now she opened the strongbox and dropped the money inside.

"Mama, what are you doing?" asked Damien.

"It's too late to take the money to the bank," she said. "So I've got to put it away."

"You're keeping it?"

"He said he wants us to have it, honey."

"But, Mama, what if he's a drug dealer or something?"

"He's not a drug dealer."

"How do you know? He looks scary, Mama. He's got these wild blue eyes."

"I know who he is, Damien," she said softly. "Willis and I went to college together. I liked him a lot. But he had a bad drinking problem. He was wonderful when he was sober and really awful when he was drunk. He never graduated from college. I always felt sorry for him. He was—well, sort of a loser. He just had a way of turning success into failure."

"A loser?" Damien questioned. "He just dropped two hundred dollars on us, Mama."

His mother shook her head. "I didn't mean just money, Damien. There's other ways of being a loser."

Damien thought for a moment. Then he said, "So why's he watching us? What does he want?"

"I don't suppose he wants anything. He's probably just lonely and too shy to pay us a visit. And the money . . . Well, Will was always doing things like that. Strange but nice things."

She slowly shut the strongbox. Damien noticed that her hands were shaking again, like the first time Damien told her about the watcher.

"So what do you think he'll do now?" asked Damien.

"He'll probably drift off and we'll never see him again," his mother replied. But she didn't sound very sure of her words.

Later that night, Damien went to his

room and read the ending of *A Tale of Two Cities*. There was no last-minute rescue. Sydney Carton went to his death. But he didn't show any sign of fear at the end. His mind was full of hope for the future.

Damien closed the book and leaned back in his chair. He thought about the tragic but wonderful ending.

What would it feel like to be that brave? Damien wondered.

He tried to go to sleep. But all kinds of things kept going through his mind. He thought about his fight with Brad, the envelope full of money, and Willis Tate's wild eyes. Damien realized he was still afraid, but he wasn't sure why.

Damien got out of bed and looked out the window. He wanted to make sure Willis Tate wasn't parked outside again. But he found that the street was empty except for a lonely figure crumpled against a light post. It was just an old man, either homeless or too drunk to find his way home.

Damien sighed. Maybe his mother was

right. Maybe Willis Tate was simply a well-meaning loner. Still, Damien was glad he was gone.

Then Damien heard a sound in the apartment—a hushed and muffled sound. He couldn't tell what it was at first. He listened very carefully.

After a minute, he realized what it was. His mother was crying.

**4** WHY IS SHE upset? Damien asked himself. His mother rarely cried. It was a little frightening to hear her now in tears.

Damien went across the hall and knocked on his mother's door. "Mama?" he called. "Mama? Are you okay?"

"Sure, honey," she said. "Come on in."

Damien walked in slowly. He found his mother sitting up in bed, propped on her pillows. There was a closed book on her lap.

"Come on over, honey," she said. "Climb up beside me and sit for a while. Remember when you were little? You'd come sit on the side of my bed and we'd talk."

The springs of the old bed wheezed when Damien sat down on the edge.

"I was scared of monsters under my bed back then," said Damien, with a slightly embarrassed grin.

His mother laughed through her tears. "That's right," she said. "I'd tell you that the monsters were just as scared of you as you were of them. And you'd go back to bed looking so brave!''

They both laughed. ''You never lectured me that there's no such thing as monsters,'' said Damien.

''I didn't want to lie to you, honey,'' said his mother. Softly she stroked his hair. ''When somebody believes in monsters, they're always real.''

Damien hesitated for a moment. Then he asked, ''Is that why you were crying? Are the 'monsters' after you too?''

His mother smiled and wiped her eyes. ''Yeah, I guess you might say they are, Damien,'' she said. ''My monsters are at school, mostly. I had a faculty meeting today. Sometimes I think it'd be easier to change every brick in that building than the minds of some of the teachers inside. They're so against anything new.''

Damien studied her face for a moment. ''That's not all that's wrong, though, is it?'' he said.

His mother just shook her head and didn't answer.

''Has it got anything to do with Willis Tate?'' Damien asked gently.

"Well, he brings back memories, I guess. The only time I've ever been out of this neighborhood was during my college years. Those were beautiful, exciting days. I met people like Will who'd been to places I'd only dreamed about. Will was a musician from New Orleans. I can't tell you how exciting he made that city sound! He said he'd take me there. We promised each other to go dancing down Bourbon Street someday."

Damien's mother hung her head tiredly. "I can't help remembering those days," she said. "Thinking about how I used to be. What would that dreamy college girl have done if she'd known she'd wind up right back here?"

Damien scarcely knew how to respond. What he finally did say seemed small comfort. "I'm sorry you had such a bad day, Mama."

"Oh, it wasn't so bad. Just a little strange, that's all." She wiped away the last of her tears and smiled.

Damien gave his mother a hug and stood up. She switched off the bed lamp.

At the doorway, Damien turned back.

"Hey, Mama," he said. "Just remember: The monsters are as scared of you as you are of them."

He couldn't see his mother's face in the dark. Yet he could sense her smile. "Thanks, Damien," she said. "I won't forget."

Damien went back to bed. He was glad that he could make his mother feel a little better. But he suspected that she hadn't told him everything. There was something more—something she couldn't talk about. And Damien was sure that it had a lot to do with Willis Tate.

* * *

The weekend came and went. Damien didn't see Willis Tate's car all that time. The whole episode started to seem as though it'd happened ages ago.

In English class on Monday, there was a big discussion on *A Tale of Two Cities.* Even those who hadn't liked the rest of the book were fascinated by the ending.

Toward the end of the period, Mr. Hall stopped the discussion. "I've been looking for a class project. Suppose we stage a play based on the closing chapters of the book? Anyone who wanted a part could have one. You don't even have to take a speaking role. You can be in the mob scene at the guillotine.

"Or you could work backstage," he added. "Design sets. Do lighting. Choose the music."

Students began to murmur excitedly.

"We could perform the play at a school assembly in a few weeks. If your families and friends are free, they can come and see it too."

Almost everyone was enthusiastic about the idea. Even Brad wanted a role. James, on the other hand, preferred to build sets.

Then Mr. Hall read off the names of the principal characters and asked for volunteers to play them. Most of the kids wanted small parts. They didn't want all the hard work of learning and rehearsing the lines.

Tara got the role of Lucie Manette, the woman Sydney Carton loved. When Mr. Hall came to Sydney Carton, Damien quickly raised his hand and got the part. Everyone agreed to start working on the play that night.

When Damien's mother got home after school, he eagerly told her the good news. By seven o'clock, he was back at school.

Mr. Hall quickly got them organized. The kids who were in charge of writing and acting sat in one corner. Those who were responsible for makeup, lighting, and sets sat nearby. They went through some books Mr. Hall had checked out from the library and discussed ideas. Only James was out of the room. He asked to go to the auditorium to start measuring for the sets.

Damien and his group had a lot of fun turning Dickens' lines into play form. The best part was reading the lines out loud to see how they sounded. Damien had won a part in a play every year since he was in sixth grade. But without a doubt, the role of Sydney Carton was the best he'd ever had.

After an hour, Mr. Hall told them they'd better quit for the night. But as Damien was about to head out the door, Mr. Hall called to him.

"Can you do me a favor, Damien?" he asked. "We'll need costumes. I know there are quite a few stored down in the prop room. They're dusty, and some need to be repaired. I'd like you to pick out whatever seems to be right. We can sort through them tomorrow. Then I'll have them cleaned and patched up."

"Sure, Mr. Hall," said Damien. He was eager for a chance to explore the prop room.

"Great. Here's the key. I'll tell the janitor where you are. I'll be here for a little while grading papers. Just drop the costumes off with me before you go."

Damien really loved the prop room. All the strange, rich costumes seemed to be haunted by the people who'd once worn them. Many of the nicer costumes had been donated by an old actress who'd gone to Wilson decades ago.

Damien ran his hand over the velvet trim on the wide sleeves of a shirt. He laughed at the knee breeches and the funny boots. But some of the stuff definitely looked like it would be right for the play.

Damien came across a couple of coats that were especially nice. One of them fit him just right.

Damien posed in front of a cracked and dingy full-length mirror. In this coat, he really seemed like Sydney Carton.

Suddenly Damien heard the sound of someone running upstairs. Who could it be? Apart from Mr. Hall, the janitor was the only person who was still supposed to be around. He surely wasn't running through the halls.

Damien dropped the costumes in a box and hurried up the stairs. He peeked down the hall just in time to see a tall, muscular man hauling away a computer. Somebody was robbing the school!

Then a voice sounded right behind Damien.

"Well, well. It's the little man himself."

Damien whirled and took in the sight of another figure holding a computer. "Stanton!" he gasped.

"Such a smart kid," Brad said with a smirk.

"Who's the little rat?"

Damien turned and found the tall man right behind him. His mouth went dry when he saw who it was: Randall Jones.

Randall was Brad's cousin. He was also one of the most feared hoods around. Randall was into anything crooked. Stealing, shaking people down, dealing drugs. Once he helped an older guy run a drug lab out of a basement apartment. There was even a rumor that Randall had killed a man.

Damien might not be afraid of Brad. But he sure was afraid of this guy.

"The little rat is Damien Blair," reported Brad. "But I bet he's not feeling much like ratting now. Are you, man? 'Cause if you do, Randall's gonna do serious harm to your pretty little mama. Right, Randall?"

And now Damien understood why

Brad was willing to be in Mr. Hall's play. Evening rehearsals gave him the perfect chance to let his cousin into the building. Then the two of them could steal everything in sight.

"You guys can't do this," said Damien. He did his best to keep his voice from shaking.

"I say we can," said Randall fiercely. "Didn't you just hear what Brad said? I seen your mama, baby boy. She walks home from the bus stop every day, doesn't she? She'd be real easy to hit." His eyes smoked with hatred.

Damien was stunned. He knew that Randall really meant it. One look at that sick grin told Damien more than any of Randall's threats. Some of the teeth were missing from that grin. Randall had lost them in fistfights. But people said that while Randall may have lost some teeth, he gave three times what he got.

"I think this little man is gonna be real quiet," whispered Randall cruelly. He saw the fear in Damien's eyes and gave another grin.

"Quiet as the grave," said Brad. He gave special emphasis to the word "grave."

With one last look at Damien, the two hoods picked up the computers. Before Damien could even think about what to do, they were out the door.

Still numb, Damien went to window and looked outside. An old car waited in the dimly lit parking lot. Randall and Brad were adding their computers to a collection already stashed in the trunk. Then they jumped into the car and sped off.

Slowly Damien's brain stirred again. He knew it was his duty to yell for the janitor and report what he'd seen. But he also knew Randall wasn't kidding. That vicious punk could harm Damien's mother long before the cops arrested him.

And even if Randall was arrested right away, he'd make bail. Weeks or months would pass before he went to trial. It would be still longer until he went to jail—if he went to jail at all. He'd have plenty of time to take his revenge.

It would be even harder to put Brad away. Since he was sixteen, he could cop a plea as a juvenile. He wasn't as big and vicious as Randall, but he was mean enough. Brad once punched a girl and broke her cheekbone. He'd do what he could to hurt Damien's mother, especially with Randall behind him.

So Damien decided to keep silent about what he'd seen. He hated himself for the decision. He couldn't imagine how he was going to play the noble Sydney Carton now. But he couldn't put his mother in danger.

Damien went to Mr. Hall's room and peered inside. Mr. Hall was still there, working at his desk. Just a minute ago, Damien had looked forward to showing Mr. Hall the costumes he'd found. Now he couldn't bring himself to do that. He placed the box inside the doorway and waved.

" 'Night, Mr. Hall," he said feebly. "I gotta go."

Mr. Hall looked up from his work. "Good night, Damien," he said. "I'll tell the janitor you're gone. Thanks."

Then Damien left the building. It was early October, and normally Damien would have enjoyed being out on such a nice night. But after what had just happened, he couldn't enjoy anything.

As he neared his apartment, he saw the police cruiser pass. The friendly cop waved as usual. Damien wanted to rush to the car and tell the cop everything. He longed to get the crushing burden off his shoulders.

But he didn't dare. He kept hearing Randall's vicious words. *She'd be real easy to hit,* Randall had said. The sick, sad truth was that there was little real safety on these streets—despite the smiling cop.

Still, Damien wished he knew someone to talk to, someone who could help him. He wondered what his father would say to him now. That smooth-faced boy in the photo had grown up on these streets. He must have faced bullies and hoods too.

Damien couldn't believe his father would hide the truth and pretend nothing had happened. But what *would* he have done? Would he have cracked those two hoods' heads together the minute they threatened him? Or would he have gone straight to the police?

Damien's mother was waiting in their small living room when he got home. "Damien, you're late," she said. "I was worried."

"Things came up," said Damien shortly.

"What's wrong, honey? You sound like you're mad at the world."

"I'm sorry, Mama. I didn't mean to sound like that. But I really hate it around here."

He sighed. Then a sudden idea struck him. "Mama, let's go someplace else," he urged. "Let's go to New Orleans, like you dreamed about doing when you were in college."

"I wish we could, Damien."

"But can't we go *someplace?*"

"Well, next year I think we'll have enough money saved to get a better apartment, honey. We can move to a nicer neighborhood."

Damien frowned. That wasn't the idea he'd had at all.

"Damien, what is it?" his mother asked again. "Did something bad happen at school?"

"Something bad's always happening, Mama. Kids threaten each other and steal things and bust things up. I really hate it."

"I know, Damien."

Damien took a long breath. "Mama, how did Dad deal with that kind of stuff? How did he keep people from pushing him around?"

A worried look crossed his mother's face. "I'll bet somebody is giving you trouble at school," she said.

"No," said Damien. He hated to lie to his mother. But he didn't know what else to do. "I just wondered about Dad. About how he handled things."

Damien's mother smiled. She was especially beautiful when she smiled.

"Charles was a really good man," she said. "That's why I married him. He was dependable and he cared about people. That kind of man isn't always easy to find. The flashy ones who promise the moon are thick as cockroaches. But Charles would be there when you needed him."

She paused for a moment and looked into her son's eyes. Damien felt like she was trying to understand what was bothering him. Maybe she knew deep down, he thought.

"I never saw your father throw a punch, Damien," she said. "I never saw him duck one either. He had so much strength about him that nobody dared lay a hand on him."

"I wish he weren't dead," said Damien sadly.

"Me too, honey," said his mother. Her voice fell to a whisper. "Me too. Every day of my life."

**5** "HEY, DID YOU hear what happened?" yelled James the moment he saw Damien the next morning. "Somebody stole some computers last night."

"No kidding?" said Damien, trying to act surprised.

"Nobody knows just when it happened," said James. "It might have been during rehearsal. Or it could have been later. I hope they prove it's later."

"What do you mean?" Damien asked. "Are they trying to nail one of us?"

"Yeah. 'Us' meaning you or me," said James.

"But we weren't the only ones in the building," Damien protested. "There were . . . Oh." Damien suddenly saw James' point.

" 'Oh' is right. You and I were the only ones who went off by ourselves. Everybody knew I was alone in the auditorium. And Mr. Hall sent you down to the prop room alone. People are hinting that maybe one of us had something to do with the robbery."

"But we didn't do it!" exclaimed Damien.

"But suppose people decide that one of us did? Just how are we supposed to prove we didn't?"

The sound of the bell broke up the conversation. Yet it certainly didn't take Damien's mind off his problems. It was starting to really hurt to have to keep silent. Yet he had to keep acting like he'd never seen anything.

After English class, Damien and Mr. Hall looked through the box of costumes. Mr. Hall was pleased with what Damien had chosen.

"I'm glad you didn't have a run-in with those thieves last night," Mr. Hall said while they sorted the clothes. "Maybe it wasn't such a good idea for me to send you alone to the prop room."

"How many computers did they get?" asked Damien. He kept his head down, so he wouldn't have to look Mr. Hall in the face.

"Six—and some software too. Insurance will probably pay for most of it.

But it'll still take a while to replace everything."

Mr. Hall didn't even ask Damien whether he'd seen anything. Damien knew the reason why. Mr. Hall trusted him. He was sure that Damien would have told somebody by now if he'd seen the thieves.

Damien felt sick with shame. What would Mr. Hall think if he knew the truth?

Damien found it hard to concentrate on his classes. Things didn't get much better when he headed out the door at the end of the day. There, across the street, sat Willis Tate in his car.

Damien's heart sank. He'd really hoped Willis Tate had paid his last visit. But this time, Damien was determined not to give in to panic. If this guy was a friend of his mother's, what was there to be scared of?

Damien crossed the street and went to the car window.

"Hi," he said timidly.

"Hi," answered Willis Tate with a

smile. His dark blue eyes looked brighter than they had before.

"Say, thanks for the money," said Damien.

"You're welcome."

"I wish you'd told me you used to know my mother. Maybe I wouldn't have taken off like that."

"Yeah, I should have told you," said Willis Tate. "I'm sorry. But I didn't think you'd believe me anyway, Damien."

Damien drew back a little. "Wait a minute. How'd you know I was Jessie Blair's son? And how come you know my name?" he asked.

"A friend told me where your mama lived. Told me about you too."

Damien stood staring at Will for a long moment. Those blue eyes seemed to hypnotize him.

The smile on Tate's face broadened. "I can tell you're looking at my eyes," he said.

"Sorry," said Damien, snapping out of his trance. "I didn't mean to stare. It's just that—"

"I know. You've never seen a black guy with blue eyes before. Well, my father's mama was white. And my grandfather on my mother's side was white too. I get my blue eyes from them."

Will looked a lot nicer when he smiled. Most of the time he had a kind of weary, lived-in face. It was like he hadn't taken good care of himself. You could tell he'd done a lot of drinking in his time.

"Do you want to hop in and go for a hamburger, Damien?" Will asked.

Immediately Damien felt his muscles tense. There was still something spooky about Willis Tate—even if his mother did know the guy.

Will's smile changed, taking on a sad look. "You don't trust me, do you, Damien?" he said. "Well, I can understand. Just shows you're smart. So how about we walk down to the hamburger place on Corning? I'll buy you a nice, big burger with onions and tomatoes and lots of special sauce."

"That's my favorite kind," said Damien. "How'd you know that?"

"I didn't know. It's *my* favorite, though. Want to go?"

Damien stopped to consider. What was the harm in just taking a walk with the guy and having a hamburger?

"Sure," said Damien.

Will parked his car and they set off together. After a moment of awkward silence, Damien tried out a question. "What's it like in New Orleans?" he asked. "Mama said you were from there."

"Oh, it's a great place," said Will. "When I was a kid, I'd watch the sailboats on Lake Pontchartrain. I remember walking along the lakefront, eating pralines. Ever taste pralines?"

"I don't think so," said Damien. "What are they?"

"They're candy made from brown sugar and pecans and butter. You can get them in any candy shop. But New Orleans—man, give me New Orleans pralines any day."

Damien's head began to fill with questions he wanted to ask Will. He wanted to know what Will had done with his life since his college days with Mama. Was he still into music? What was he doing here now? Did he . . . well, did he still care about Mama?

But he knew it was rude to ask personal questions like that. That didn't seem to stop the adults in the neighborhood from doing it, though. For instance, a lot of people kept asking his mother why she didn't get married again.

"You're such a pretty thing," old Mrs. Hawthorne was always saying. "It's just a crime you're not married!"

Damien's mother always smiled and said nothing. Damien, too, sometimes wondered why his mother never remarried. She went out on dates from time to time, and most of the men seemed okay to Damien. But the dates never turned into anything very serious. Damien figured his mother had never found another man as good as Charles Blair. And she wouldn't settle for less.

Damien glanced at Will. Those blue eyes now seemed kind and warm. Maybe Damien could get advice about his problems from this man. Damien felt like he had to talk to *somebody* or go crazy.

"Did you grow up in a tough neighborhood like this?" asked Damien.

"Not like this, but it was tough enough."

"So did anybody ever push you around? I mean like when you were my age?"

Will laughed. "Oh, yeah, sure. That's the way it is with kids, I guess."

"Did you ever get into fights?"

"Yeah. I was a musician—kind of artistic, you know? You can imagine how that sat with some of the cleats."

"Cleats?"

"The jocks. I beat up a few faces and got my own beaten up too."

Well, there it was. Here was Damien's opening if he wanted it. But how much could he ask this guy? Damien wondered. How much could he tell him?

They were just outside the hamburger place when Damien stopped and looked up at Will. "When you were a kid," Damien asked nervously, "what would you have done if you saw a crime? Like somebody ripping off stuff. Would you have told the cops?''

Will thought carefully. ''Well, I was in trouble with the law myself as a kid. So I don't guess I'd have told. But I was no good, Damien. I was a serious drunk by the time I was seventeen. I'm not the best guy to ask.''

''What if somebody threatened you?''

Will laughed. ''That would have made it different. I was a tough punk and hated getting pushed around. I might have gone to the cops just for spite.''

''But suppose somebody . . . suppose they threatened to hurt your mother?''

A strange look crossed Willis Tate's face. His blue eyes suddenly blazed with anger.

''Why do you want to know, Damien?'' he asked sternly.

Damien edged away. ''No reason,'' he said. ''I—I'm sorry if I got out of line.''

''What is this stuff, Damien? Has somebody been threatening you? Or Jessie?'' asked Will.

"No. I just ask too many questions sometimes. I'm sorry."

Will stared at Damien silently, studying him.

"Listen," said Damien, "maybe a hamburger isn't such a good idea. I mean, it was nice of you to offer. But I just wouldn't feel right about it."

The anger in Will's face slowly faded. His face and eyes softened. To Damien's relief, a trace of that warm, sad smile came back.

"Yeah, Damien, I understand," he said softly. "Maybe some other time."

With a shy wave, Damien turned away. His mind was in a whirlwind, so he didn't see Tara until he almost ran into her.

"Hey, Tara," he said.

Tara glanced back down the street. "Who was that?" She gestured with her chin.

"Oh. That guy I was with?"

"Yeah. Him."

"His name's Willis Tate."

"So who's Willis Tate?"

"An old friend of my mother's,"

Damien answered. "He was the one who was following me around, Tara."

Tara glanced back again. "Are you sure he's okay? He looks this side of strange."

"Well, he seems okay," said Damien with a shrug. "I don't know that much about him," he confessed.

"Look, Damien, does your mother still know this guy? I mean, he looks like the kind that's into drugs or sleazy movies or something."

"I don't think . . . " Damien started to protest. Then he admitted, "I don't know what to think about him. He keeps hanging around, and I don't know why. He even gave Mama and me some money yesterday."

Tara shook her head. "Nobody gives people money unless they want something back," she said. "So what does he want, you suppose?"

"I just don't know. Maybe he's wiping out some old debt. Anyway, he acts like he feels guilty about something. Like he's trying to make up for something he did."

"Well, watch your back," said Tara. "You don't need his kind of trouble."

Damien felt like laughing. Willis Tate's kind of trouble was nothing compared to—

Suddenly Damien couldn't keep his secret to himself any longer. He was tired of worrying about Stanton and his cousin. He was sick of wondering whether his mother was safe at that very minute.

He stopped dead in his tracks and turned to Tara. "Tara," he said, "can you keep a really big secret?"

**6** TARA STARED AT Damien for a second. Then she said, "Yeah, I can keep a secret."

"You promise?" Damien asked.

"I promise."

"You won't tell, no matter what?"

Tara looked both annoyed and a little frightened. "Come on, Damien," she said. "What is it?"

"Well, I know who stole the computers," Damien confessed. "I saw them."

"Are you serious?"

"Yeah. It was Brad Stanton and his cousin, Randall Jones."

"Well, why haven't you told anybody?" Tara demanded.

Damien sighed. "They said if I told, they'd hurt my mother. They said they could hit her real easy. And they could too."

Tara gripped Damien's arm. "Damien! You're kidding! I mean, they wouldn't . . . " She trailed off.

"Yes they would, Tara. And that's what's got me shook. You know those stories about Randall Jones killing a guy. And I don't think they're just stories."

Tara stared down at the pavement. Then she looked up at Damien, her eyes full of worry. "Damien, what *are* you going to do?"

Damien laughed bitterly. "Man, I was hoping you'd tell me. I can't tell the cops. Randall will do what he says. He's been stealing cars since he was thirteen. Since he was fifteen, he's been sending people to the hospital. Now he's set on sending 'em straight to the graveyard. I can't protect Mama from somebody like that. Neither can the cops."

"Maybe they could," Tara said.

Damien shrugged. "Maybe. But 'maybe' isn't good enough. If Randall Jones knew I ratted, he'd be after Mama."

"The cops might bust Jones and Stanton for something else. Their kind is always making trouble."

"I hope so," said Damien. But the tone of his voice showed he didn't have much hope. "Anyway, you promised you wouldn't say a word, right?" he added.

Tara nodded. "Yeah," she said. "I don't feel good about it, but I promised. I guess it's like my grandma says: Sometimes you can't do the right thing even when you want to. Sometimes the world won't let you."

As Damien walked on home, he thought over what Tara had said. She hadn't had any answers. But he was still glad he'd told her. Sharing his problem with somebody made it easier to bear.

\* \* \*

Early that evening, while Damien and his mother were eating dinner, the doorbell rang. Damien went to the door. He looked out the peephole and saw a delivery boy.

When Damien opened the door, the boy handed him a box wrapped with a yellow ribbon. Damien brought the box inside.

"What is it, honey?" his mother asked.

"I'm not sure," said Damien, setting the box on the table. "But I got another hunch, Mama, and it's one I'd bet on. That box isn't for me."

Damien's mother smiled and reached for a note attached to the package. When she read it, a startled look passed over her face.

"Who's it from, Mama?" asked Damien.

"Willis Tate," she said in a quiet voice.

"Well, open it."

Damien's mother glanced at him and then opened the box. There was a pound of delicious-looking sweets inside.

"Pralines," his mother said. "These sure bring back the memories. Will used to feed me these things like they were soda crackers."

"Hey, he must really like you," said Damien. "Maybe he wants to start up with you again."

His mother shook her head. "I don't think so, honey. Willis and I had a nice time for a while, but he's no fool. He knows we could never get together in a million years."

Then a sly grin spread across her face.

"Besides, these pralines aren't for me. Remember what I told you about those hunches of yours, Damien?"

She handed Damien the note and he, too, read it.

*Damien,*

*Not as good as the ones from New Orleans. But close enough to give you a taste of the real thing.*

*Willis Tate*

Damien was taken aback. "Why's he giving me stuff?" he said. "I don't even know the guy."

His mother stared out the window for a minute. Then she turned back to Damien. "He's probably just lonely, honey," she said. "I don't imagine he has folks of his own anymore. He came from a nice family, but too many of them had problems with drinking. Will's father died young from liver disease.

"And Will pretty much drank his life

away too," she added. "After college, he wrote some bad checks. Even landed in prison."

She sighed and closed the praline box. "So I guess he realizes he's lost his chance for a family of his own. And he sees that you don't have a daddy, so . . . well, you know."

Damien acted as though he understood. But he couldn't shake the feeling that his mother wasn't telling the whole truth.

Later, Damien's mother asked him about the stolen computers. "It was all over my school how Wilson High was robbed. Any talk about who did it, honey?"

"No," said Damien, pretending to be busy with his homework. "It really wasn't that big a deal."

"What do you mean, Damien?" his mother said. "Those thieves took six computers and a load of software."

Damien sat back and angrily slammed his book closed. "Come on, Mama! That's just life around here. People rob stores.

They shoot at each other. They deal drugs. That's just the way it is. Only a fool worries about it, because worrying's sure not going to change anything."

"Honey, what's got into you? That's not you talking."

"I'm not a little kid anymore, Mama," Damien snapped. "I can't be hiding under the covers, make-believing that the monsters aren't there if I can't see them."

Then Damien looked up and saw the pain on his mother's face. His anger died.

"Mama, I'm sorry. I didn't mean to get mad at you. Look, I hate what they did at school. But you get sick of banging your head against a brick wall. It's like this book I've been reading. The evil people always seem to be on top. If you're bad enough, nobody can stop you."

"Damien, don't let bitterness eat you up."

"I can't help it, Mama. It just seems like the rich feed off the poor and the poor feed off each other. I guess it's always that way."

"But what about Sydney Carton?" his

mother asked.

"What?"

"Well, you're the one who brought up *A Tale of Two Cities,*" his mother pointed out. "Sydney Carton gave up his life to help his friends. And I've heard you practicing that speech of his just before he dies. Remember? 'It is a far, far better thing that I do, than I have ever done . . . ' "

" 'It is a far, far better rest I go to, than I have ever known,' " said Damien, finishing the quote. "Yeah, that's a really fine speech.

"But how many Sydney Cartons have you ever actually met, Mama?" he continued. "Real people aren't like that. They're selfish. People around here would never risk their lives to help somebody else."

"Don't be too sure, Damien," said his mother. "And I'll tell you another thing. Treat somebody like a crook and you'll get robbed for sure. Expect something better and they might just give it to you."

Damien let the argument rest there.

But he still wasn't convinced. That night at rehearsal, he just couldn't put his heart into the role of Sydney Carton. Suddenly Dickens' whole story seemed cheap and unreal to Damien.

To make matters worse, Brad kept goofing off and causing trouble. Sometimes he'd toss a sneer Damien's way. He looked happy with himself—too happy for Damien's taste. Damien wondered what new stunt Brad had pulled. But maybe he really didn't want to know.

Later that night, Damien sat in his room leafing through a book. But nothing on the page interested him.

Then he looked out the window. He rose to his feet when he noticed Will Tate's car sitting by the curb.

He's crazy, Damien decided. He's just a sad, crazy guy. Willis Tate was like those poor fools on the street—the ones who said they'd been to Jupiter.

Damien went to bed, but he couldn't sleep. He read the last part of *A Tale of Two Cities* again. Was his mother right?

Were there really brave people in the world?

Then Damien remembered what Mr. Hall had told him. He said that nobody could tell Damien the answer to that question. *It's all a matter of experience,* Mr. Hall had said.

Damien decided he'd had enough experience. Now he knew and the answer was simple. If you couldn't see that kind of courage in yourself, then it probably wasn't in other people either. Sydney Carton was just a character. He was a beautiful character, but he did things real people never do.

Damien put the book aside and thought about his father. Maybe he hadn't been brave either.

But something in Damien rebelled at that thought. Even if Charles Blair hadn't been a super hero, he'd been a good man.

And how different life would be if he'd lived! Charles Blair would have gotten his degree in engineering. Then he would have moved his family out of this neighborhood—maybe even out of this city.

But when he died, he didn't even have any life insurance. So Damien's mother had been struggling ever since just to make ends meet. On a teacher's salary, that wasn't easy.

I hate that hit-and-run driver, thought Damien. I hope whoever did kill my father has suffered like nobody else on earth.

Suddenly Damien sat bolt upright, his eyes wide. He ran to the window and stared at the black sedan.

Who is Willis Tate? he wondered desperately. What is it that Mama won't tell me about him?

Could Will have been the hit-and-run driver? Was that the missing piece in the puzzle? Was that the reason Will felt so guilty and was trying to force his help on them?

Damien frantically pulled on his clothes. The whole thing now seemed horribly clear. Willis Tate had been trying to visit his old girlfriend that night. But he was drunk as usual and ran down Damien's father.

Yet was it true? Could Damien really believe such a thing?

Damien was shaking as he ran from his room. He swung open the door and sprinted down the stairs, slipping and skidding as he went. He dashed outside, blindly rushing toward the parked car.

Finally as he neared the car, he slowed. He took a deep breath and tried to calm himself.

"Willis!" he called out, his voice trembling.

"Damien! You shouldn't be out on the street at this hour," Will scolded.

Damien stood outside the car window. "You've got to tell me!" he exclaimed. "You've got to tell me who you are! You've got to tell me why you're here!"

Will's expression became troubled. "I'm an old friend, Damien," he said. "That's all."

"That's *not* all! You and I both know it's not!"

"What do you mean?"

Damien's breath caught for a moment. "Did you kill him?" he cried out suddenly. "Did you kill my father?"

A look of horror crossed Will's face. "Damien, no," he whispered. "Lord, no."

There was a world of shock and sadness in those words. But was Will shocked that Damien could think something so wild about him? Or was he shocked that Damien had discovered the truth?

"You've got to tell me!" pleaded Damien. "How can I think anything except the worst if you don't tell me?"

Will shook his head wearily. "I can't," he said. "Not now. Not like this."

Without another word, Willis Tate started the car. He drove off slowly into the darkness.

Still shaking with rage and confusion, Damien watched the car disappear. Then a new thought hit him. Whatever Will's secret was, his mother must have known it too. She'd known it all these years and hadn't told him. If Damien couldn't trust her, who could he trust?

As Damien walked wearily back to the apartment, the world seemed a more terrible place than it ever had before.

**7** DAMIEN COULDN'T LOOK at his mother during breakfast the next morning. All he could think about was the secret that she'd kept from him for so many years.

It didn't take long for his mother to see something was wrong. "Are you sick, honey?" she asked.

Damien shook his head. "I'm okay," he said.

But he actually did feel sick. He felt like he'd been poisoned with doubt and mistrust.

Once he nearly asked his mother, point-blank, who Will Tate really was. But yesterday she hadn't told him the truth. Today would be no different.

Damien glanced up at those kind, brown eyes for an instant. Then he hastily looked away again.

How could she have lied to me? he wondered miserably.

As early as possible, Damien hurried to school. He was eager to talk to James. James usually knew just what to say to stop Damien from worrying. And Damien was sick of worrying.

But James wasn't at his locker. However, it didn't take long to find out where he was. As Damien started down the hall, Terry Stamper, another kid in his class, yelled at him.

"Hey, Damien! Did you hear? James Moran got busted!"

"Busted?" Damien gasped. "What for?"

"For taking the computers," said Terry breathlessly. "Boy, you shoulda been on our block last night. It was crawling with cops! Everybody was out in the street. James' mother was screaming and hollering. And his sisters and brother were yelling too."

"But James didn't do it," Damien said in a choked voice. "I mean, he couldn't have. Not James."

"He did it, all right," said Terry. "The cops found some software stashed in his house. But the computers were gone. I guess the guy he stole them for got them already."

"James didn't do it!" Damien shouted.

"Hey, I know you guys are real tight," said Terry. "But face it. The janitor saw him alone in the auditorium that night."

"He was helping build the set for our show!"

"Yeah, that's what he wanted everybody to think. But it was him, all right. The cops got tipped off by an anonymous phone call."

Then Damien caught sight of Brad. He'd been standing there, listening. Now he came swaggering over.

"Who'd have figured?" said Brad, grinning right in Damien's face. "Old James Moran. Boot-licking, yes-ma'aming, poh-lite James. Imagine him turning out to be a grubbing little thief. Life's sure peculiar."

Damien stared at Brad with pure hatred. It was plain what had happened. When people got suspicious of James, Brad saw his chance. He stuck James with some cheap software, then tipped off the cops. It was perfect. With an innocent guy nailed, Brad and his cousin were home free.

Terry walked away, and Damien found himself alone with Brad.

"It burns your guts, doesn't it, man?" Brad said with a grin. "Can't do a thing about it either. Maybe now you'll think twice about taking me on again. Stuff like that leads to nasty paybacks."

Damien watched Brad stroll off, chuckling.

Damien sank down onto a bench. James. He shook his head. What was poor James going to do?

Like Damien, James had no father. But unlike Damien's mother, Mrs. Moran wasn't educated. She had to clean houses and businesses six days a week to keep her family going.

But Mrs. Moran was proud. She kept a nice, clean apartment for her four children. And nothing was more important to her than her kids. She was determined that they'd all be successful. Damien couldn't imagine the pain this must be causing her.

Damien was dizzy with confusion as he went to his first class. He met Tara in the hall. For a minute they just stared at one another.

Damien could see that Tara had been crying. Her eyes were puffy and red-rimmed. She was a close friend of James, just like Damien. The three of them had hung around together since they were in first grade.

"Oh, Damien!" she whispered.

"Yeah," he said.

"It's so unfair. It's gonna kill James' mother!"

"You won't tell, will you?" Damien asked.

Tara shook her head. "I promised not to, and I won't," she said. "But what are you going to do about it, Damien? You can't just let this happen to James."

Tara waited for an answer from Damien. But he couldn't give her an answer—at least not the one she wanted. He saw the hope in her eyes flicker and burn out. Silently Tara turned and hurried away.

Damien's heart felt like a stone. As he walked toward English class, Brad fell in step beside him. "Hey, little man," he whispered. "What you figure old James is doing right now? You figure they put him in lockup with some serious killers, maybe?"

Damien stared straight ahead. His mouth went dry.

"Lockup's not so bad," Brad continued with a vicious laugh. "Randall says it's just like a hotel. And old Randall should know. He's been in so many times, they got a bunk with his name on it. But Randall's smart. He's never in for long."

Strange noises filled Damien's brain. He heard a roaring, as if the sea were trapped in his skull. There was a pounding too, like an army marching through his head. He felt his hands clench and form into fists.

Suddenly Damien turned. He grabbed Brad's shoulders, forcing him against the wall. Brad looked startled by the unexpected violence.

"All right," said a teacher coming down the hall. "Break it up or you're both on detention."

Damien drew back, releasing Brad. Too angry to speak, he hurried away to class.

During English, Damien stared at James' desk and thought about where James was now. He thought, too, about Freeman's Grocery and the bin of apples out front. Seems like every kid in the neighborhood had stolen an apple from that bin. Every kid except James. Whenever anybody ragged him about that, he'd look kind of embarrassed. But no matter how hard they rode him, James never stole one of those apples.

"Mr. Hall," said Damien, "I'm feeling sick. May I be excused?"

"Of course," said Mr. Hall.

Damien grabbed his books. A railroad train was racing inside his head, gathering steam. He rushed from the room, breaking into a run in the hall.

In front of the pay phone, Damien stopped. For a moment he recalled his angry suspicions about his mother and Willis Tate. But suddenly he saw that whatever Will may have done, his mother wasn't involved. She'd loved Charles

Blair—just as she loved Damien.

His hands shaking, Damien punched in the number of his mother's school.

"Mama," he said when he got her on the line, "I saw the guys who stole the computers the other night. It was Brad Stanton and his cousin, Randall Jones."

The words came gushing out now. "I kept quiet about it because they said they'd hurt you. But then they went and framed James Moran. Now I'm going crazy. I don't know what to do. Mama, you've gotta tell me what to do."

"Honey, stay where you are," his mother said soothingly. "I'll get somebody to cover my class and be there in twenty minutes."

Damien headed outside and waited. Time seemed to creep by at a snail's pace. But finally his mother pulled up in a cab. She opened the door and called out, "Jump in, honey!" She hugged Damien when he was inside.

"Where are we going, Mama?" Damien asked.

"To the police station," she said.

Damien swallowed hard. It was the answer he was expecting—and dreading.

The officer who met them at the station was Sergeant Alvarez. When Damien was little, the good-natured Cuban had let him ride in his cruiser. Now Sergeant Alvarez led Damien and his mother to a desk and listened to Damien's story.

"You're not just saying this because your friend is in trouble, eh?" he asked when Damien was finished.

"No," Damien said. "Brad Stanton and Randall Jones stole the computers. I saw them."

"Well, Randall's certainly had a string of arrests," said Sergeant Alvarez. "Some of them for theft."

"Everybody says he killed a guy once," said Damien.

"Could be. Easier to say than to prove."

"Are you going to arrest them and lock them up now?" asked Damien.

"Well, Damien, I'm not going to lie to you. Because of your report, we'll investigate. But I can't promise that

Randall Jones will be off the streets by tonight."

Damien looked at his mother worriedly. "He's going to be out there, Mama," he said.

# 8

DAMIEN'S MOTHER PUT her arm around her son and gave his shoulders a squeeze.

"It's going to be all right," she said. "You'll see. Now don't worry."

"We'll keep an eye out for you," promised Sergeant Alvarez. "Randall Jones isn't going to get away with hurting anybody. And we have ways of tracing those computers even if he's already sold them. It'll just take time."

On the way home, Damien looked out the cab window. For some reason, he was reminded of the ride to his father's funeral. He wasn't even three at the time. Yet he remembered wearing his little blue suit, clutching his mother's hand. He remembered the coffin at the church too—and trying to understand why his father was so still.

Damien wondered what made him think of those things now. Why did he feel like that little boy again?

He looked over at his mother. She was a slim and delicate woman. But now she looked like a tower of strength. That must be the reason, Damien figured. She made Damien feel that he wasn't so grown-up after all.

"I hope Sergeant Alvarez was right," he said. "I hope they can keep Randall away from you."

"Don't worry, Damien," said his mother calmly. "I'll be fine."

"I felt so awful, Mama—about you and James both. I hope they let James out quick."

"I'm sure they will."

Damien sighed sadly. "I should have come and told you right away," he said.

"You didn't know what to do," said his mother reassuringly. "Sometimes it's hard to know what to do—especially around here."

"Do you suppose Dad would have been proud of what we did?"

"You bet, honey."

Damien felt a small shiver at the thought of Randall's anger. "Dad wouldn't have been scared, would he?"

Damien's mother smiled. "Oh, he'd have been scared. But he still would have done the right thing. You know, it isn't hard to do what's right when you're not afraid. But when you're scared to death and do the right thing anyway—well, I guess that's all bravery really is."

\* \* \*

Later that night, Damien was sitting on the front steps. He felt better being able to keep an eye on the street. And the sight of the police car that kept passing by made him feel safer too.

Something else had drawn Damien outside. When the black sedan pulled up to the curb, Damien knew what he'd been waiting for.

Willis Tate got out and walked over to Damien.

"Look, Damien. About last night . . . " he began.

"What about it?" Damien prodded. His heart was a tangle of emotions. Mostly he just felt tired of worrying about things.

"I didn't kill your father, Damien,"

said Will. "I understand why you think so, but I didn't. When your father was killed, I was doing three to five years for larceny."

Damien looked down at the sidewalk for a moment. Then he met Will's gaze. "I don't know what to believe," said Damien.

"Yeah, I know. But you can check it out for yourself. I've done some rotten things. But manslaughter's not one of them."

Will's voice sounded sincere. Damien wanted to believe him. But he was too troubled to say anything for a moment.

"Look, just think about what I said," said Will. "Maybe later we can talk."

Then Will returned to his car and drove away.

\* \* \*

At school the next day, Damien met James on the way to class. James still looked badly shaken. Damien knew he'd lived through a terrible nightmare.

"It was awful," James told Damien quietly. "It was the worst thing that ever happened to me. I couldn't believe it . . . I couldn't believe it. Man, they kept asking me all these questions. Didn't matter if I told them a hundred times what I'd been doing that night. They kept wanting to hear it again."

Damien shook his head. He didn't know what to say.

"I've got to hand it to Stanton and his cousin," James continued. "They tricked me good. They caught me on the way home from school and pushed me around. I thought they were just roughing me up for no reason. But they were really trying to slip that software in my school bag."

Shame welled up inside of Damien. "I'm sorry, James," he said. "Look, I guess you must have wondered why I didn't go to the cops right away."

James seemed embarrassed too. "Hey, man. I understand. I would've been scared of those guys too. The important thing is that you—"

Damien cut in. "I was scared, all right. See, Jones threatened my mother." Damien couldn't keep his voice from shaking. "He said he'd hurt her if I told."

James stared at Damien with a curious expression. Damien held his breath, wondering what James would say next.

Then James nodded. "I guess it's been hard for both of us, huh?"

Damien smiled with relief. "Yeah," he said. "I guess."

"Well, thanks," said James, slapping Damien on the shoulder. "Thanks for coming through."

The happy grin on Damien's face died. Swaggering down the hall towards them was Brad Stanton.

Brad pulled up short when he saw James. "What are you doing out, man?" he asked James.

James said nothing. He just stared at Brad accusingly.

Damien could see a slow realization pass over Brad's face. Brad now knew the truth. He knew that Damien had gone to the police.

Suddenly Brad wheeled on Damien. "You played it all wrong, man," Brad said fiercely. "James didn't have a record. They would've gone easy on him. You could've been a smart boy and kept quiet."

Brad shook his head. "But no. You had to play Boy Scout and make trouble for Randall and me. Now the cops'll be all over both of us. And that won't go down good with Randall at all. You blew it."

"Don't make more trouble, Brad," Damien said. "You're in enough trouble already."

"Trouble?" Brad snarled. "You don't know the meaning of that word, Blair. But you're gonna learn." Then he hurried away.

James shook his head. "Why's he so full of hate?" he asked.

"I don't know," said Damien. "I just don't know."

Damien was glad not to be carrying around secrets anymore. All the same, he was scared. Hoods like Randall Jones struck whenever you least expected, like rattlesnakes in the underbrush. By the time you saw them coming, it was often too late.

When Damien left school that day, he saw Willis Tate standing on the sidewalk.

"Feel like a hamburger, maybe?" asked Will with a smile.

Damien smiled back. Will had told him to think over their conversation about the hit-and-run accident. Well, he'd thought it through. His mama had warned him about playing hunches. Still, Damien just didn't feel this strange but kindly man had been his father's killer.

"Sounds good," said Damien.

They talked as they strolled down the block.

"You live around here?" asked Damien.

"Yeah," said Willis. "Moved here pretty recently."

"What do you do?"

"I'm a musician. I play the horn in a couple clubs around here."

"What kind of horn?"

"Clarinet."

Damien suddenly remembered the photo of his mother by the door. She'd been holding a clarinet. Will's clarinet.

"It's not a bad living," Will added.

"Must not be," Damien agreed. "That's a pretty cool car you drive."

Will grinned. "Let's just say it keeps me in burgers," he said.

They sat down at a table and ordered burgers with fries. As they ate, Damien told Will about his run-in with Brad and Randall. He also explained his hard decision to go to the police. Will listened with interest and concern.

"You did the right thing," said Will.

"Yeah, but I'm worried about Mama."

Will's forehead wrinkled slightly. "So am I, Damien," he said.

Damien looked up from his hamburger. "You like Mama a lot, don't you?" he said.

Will chuckled a little. "Well, she's a fine woman. But I'm not in love with her, if that's what you mean. Not now."

Damien was a little disappointed. He was starting to like Will. And it was nice to have a grown man—other than a teacher—to talk with. Since Damien's grandfather had died, he'd rarely had that chance.

"So how're you doing in school, Damien?" asked Will.

"Okay," said Damien shyly.

Will chuckled. "Don't give me that. I know you're doing better than okay."

"How do you know?"

"I just know. Man, you can even tell by looking at you that you're smart. So what kind of grades you get?"

"A's, mostly," Damien said softly.

Will laughed. "A's, mostly!" he echoed. "You're being shy again, man. Come on. Somebody asks me to blast my horn, they don't hear a little squeak. I'll bet you're a straight-A student."

Damien ducked his head and grinned. It was true. How did this guy seem to know so much about him?

"Good grades are nothing to be ashamed of," continued Will. "You want something to be ashamed of, look at my old grades. It's a wonder I ever got into college.

"But I was always messing up when I was a kid," Will admitted. "I'd skip school to watch the boats on the lake. Or I'd sneak down to the French Quarter and watch the jazzmen play. Sometimes I'd hide out in Jackson Square and watch the fire-eaters and listen to the saxophones."

"Did you graduate from high school?"

"Yeah, barely. Then I was off to college for a couple of years . . . "

Will let the sentence dangle. Damien could tell he didn't want to talk about what had happened after that. He sure didn't want to talk about his time in prison. Damien couldn't blame him.

Damien studied Will's face. Funny, he'd thought Will was a scary-looking guy at first. Now Damien could see that behind his ragged edges, Will was handsome.

"Say, Will, my English class is putting on a play Wednesday after next. It's based on *A Tale of Two Cities* by Charles Dickens. You want to come?"

"I'd like that fine. You have a part in

it?"

"Yeah. Sydney Carton. He's sort of the hero. At the end of the play, he gives up his life to save somebody else."

Damien paused. Then he asked carefully, "Do you think people really do that kind of thing?"

"What? Sacrifice themselves for other people?"

"Yeah."

"Well, that's what you and your mother did, isn't it? I mean, it's not like you gave up your lives. But both of you put your safety on the line to help a friend. Isn't that the same thing?"

Damien was startled. He didn't know what to say. He hadn't thought about it that way. But now that Will said so, it seemed to be true.

As Damien watched Will munch away at his hamburger, he found himself liking him more and more. Even so, Damien's mind flooded over with unanswered questions.

"Will," he blurted without stopping to think, "why are you hanging around?"

Will looked up at Damien. His blue eyes looked troubled.

Damien realized how rude the question had sounded. Hastily he added, "It's not that I mind. I mean, you're a real cool guy. But you keep buying me stuff. And you spend time talking to me. What's it all about?"

Will was quiet for a long moment. "I want to tell you," he said at last. "But I've got to take care of something first." Then, after a pause, Will added, "Soon. I'll tell you real soon."

They said nothing as they finished eating their hamburgers. The silence was full of mystery.

**9** ALL THAT NIGHT, a police car kept passing by the apartment. Willis Tate, too, sat parked in his sedan across the street for a time. Damien went to sleep feeling a little more sure of his mother's safety.

At breakfast the next morning, Damien's mother asked him how the play was going. "Okay. Especially since Brad Stanton didn't show up for practice last night. Still doesn't feel like we'll be ready in another week and a half though."

"I've heard you reading your lines. You'll be fantastic. I can't wait to see you."

Damien grinned. Suddenly he remembered his invitation to Willis. "Say, Mama, Will's coming too!"

"He is?" she asked.

"Uh-huh," said Damien. He tried to watch his mother's face, but she ducked her head. Was she smiling? Damien couldn't tell.

Damien wasn't at all sure how his mother and Will felt about each other. Once they seemed to have been very close. But how did they feel now? Was there any chance of them getting together—even though they both said they wouldn't?

Damien was even more confused about his own feelings. Did he want Mama and Will to get together or didn't he? It would be nice to have a grown-up guy around to talk to and do things with. Yet was Will the right guy for Mama? All Damien knew was that he couldn't help liking Willis Tate.

As Damien helped gather up the breakfast dishes, his mother said, "Oh. Nearly forgot. We're having a guest for Sunday dinner."

Damien's heart took a leap. His mother must have asked Willis Tate! "Yeah?" he asked eagerly. "Who?"

"Ben Winters. You've met him before. He teaches sixth grade at my school."

Damien's heart sank a little. "Oh, yeah. I remember him," he said quietly. Actually, Damien had liked Ben a lot. Ben was generous with kids. In fact, he volunteered his time to coach baseball and basketball. He was a nice enough guy. So why did Damien suddenly feel disappointed?

"Well," said Damien, trying to act enthusiastic, "is this a *date?*"

His mother laughed. "Ben and I've gotten to be good friends this year, that's all. I thought it might be nice to have him over."

Damien and his mother stacked the dishes in silence. Then Damien said, "What would you think about having Will over to dinner some night?"

Damien's mother glanced at him. She seemed suddenly uneasy.

"I don't mean a date," added Damien. "I'm just talking about the three of us getting together."

"Maybe," she said. "We'll have to see." That was all she said.

After the dishes were finished, Damien watched his mother walk down the street to the bus stop. Damien guessed that she probably was afraid even though she didn't look it. But the police car was cruising nearby, its driver keeping careful watch.

Damien felt reassured. Even Randall couldn't get past this sort of protection.

That morning at school, Damien told Tara about his conversation with Will the afternoon before.

"So he turned out to be a pretty good guy, huh?" said Tara.

"Yeah," said Damien. "He's cool and he really listens. But I wish he'd say why he's hanging around. I can't figure out why he's so interested in *me.*"

"Maybe he wants to get in good with your mama again," said Tara with a shrug.

"Could be. But I don't feel like he's using me. Only . . . "

"Only what?" Tara prompted.

"Well, he's got some kind of secret," said Damien. "He said he'd tell me what it is. But I don't know if he really will."

Tara shook her head. "Doesn't sound too good, Damien. Most secrets are kind of ugly."

Damien thought about Tara's words on the way to his locker. He supposed she was right. Most secrets covered up something wrong or bad.

But sometimes people did wrong things for good reasons. When he kept quiet about the computers, it was because he feared for his mother's safety.

Was Willis Tate's secret like that too? Was he keeping it to protect somebody? Maybe even to protect Damien?

When Damien arrived at his locker, he found the padlock broken. He hurriedly opened the door and saw that all his books were gone. A typed note was taped on the inside.

*You won't be needing your books again. Dead people don't read.*

A couple of other students had spotted Damien's busted locker. Now they drew closer and read the note over his shoulder.

"Man, I'd start packing a gun if I were you," said one kid with a shudder. The other kid just shook his head and whistled.

On his way to class, Damien kept an

eye out for Brad. He soon found Stanton in the hall, laughing it up with some other hoods.

"Where'd you put my books?" Damien demanded. He waved the note in Brad's face.

"I don't know what you're talking about," growled Brad.

"Okay, pea brain. I'll say it real slow so even you'll understand it. You broke into my locker and took my stuff. *Now where'd you put my books?*"

Brad straightened up and glared at Damien. "You making more trouble for me? You just try it and you'll get double whatever you got coming!" Brad threatened. "Now get out of my face. Go whine to the principal about your freakin' books."

Brad stomped away. Damien was about to follow him when Tara and James came by. They stopped Damien and asked what was wrong. In a voice still shaking with rage, Damien told them about the raid on his locker.

James and Tara managed to calm him

down. Tara even offered to share her books with Damien until he got his back. Then they walked on to English class.

Mr. Hall began class by handing back their papers about *A Tale of Two Cities.* He went over some points. Then he asked them for any final thoughts about the book.

"I loved the ending, where Sydney Carton gives up his life," said one girl. "But nobody would write a book like that today."

"Nobody would *do* a thing like that today," said another student.

"Yeah," said yet another student. "Imagine a guy offering to get his head chopped off in place of someone else on *this* street!"

Several students laughed in harsh agreement. The discussion began to grow lively. Most of the class agreed that Sydney Carton's self-sacrifice wasn't realistic. A few thought differently.

Damien listened to the debate. He remembered how Sydney Carton's death had once seemed like a fairy tale to him.

Now he wasn't so sure.

Damien raised his hand. "Dying in somebody's place isn't the only kind of bravery there is," he said. "And there *are* brave people around—even in this neighborhood. Look at some of the parents. They work day and night just to give their kids a better chance in life.

"And what about the doctors and nurses down at the clinic? Don't you think they could make more money in another neighborhood? They're just as scared as the rest of us about being poor and getting hurt. But they stay here in spite of that."

Damien looked around. He realized that everyone was staring at him. He suddenly felt very self-conscious.

Damien stumbled on. "There's still one thing I don't understand though. When Sydney Carton goes to his death, he's not scared at all. He's just filled with all these great thoughts about the future. I mean, I can see taking a terrible risk and being scared. But to face up to danger and not even blink?"

Mr. Hall nodded slowly. "It does seem extraordinary, Damien," he said. "Maybe that's something more than bravery."

Later that day, James delivered some startling news to Damien. "Hey, did you hear what happened?" James asked. "The cops found a bunch of stuff in this old garage Randall uses. Now there's a warrant out for his arrest. And Brad's skipped out of school. Guess they must be holed up somewhere together, huh?"

"Yeah, guess so," said Damien. He knew he should be happy about the news. But he couldn't help worrying.

As Damien left school that day, his mind returned to what he'd said in English class. And he thought about Mr. Hall. Damien had wanted to say that he thought Mr. Hall was brave too. Brave for putting so much love into his work, even when nobody else seemed to care. Brave for holding kids to certain standards and seeing that they learned. Even brave for showing that it wasn't stupid to love a good book.

But Damien knew Mr. Hall would have

been embarrassed by those words. So he'd kept silent.

As Damien walked on home, Brad and Randall grew farther and farther from his mind. He started thinking about his part in the play. Carefully he went over his lines.

Damien was so wrapped up in the play that he didn't see the car speeding toward him as he started across a bridge. He didn't notice it until he heard the roar of the high-powered engine.

With a start, Damien looked up. And finally he saw the ton and a half of steel— coming straight for him.

# 10

IT WAS RANDALL at the wheel, of course. Randall smiling that awful, jagged smile of his.

Damien glanced wildly around. At once he saw it was hopeless to run. So he did the only thing he could. Desperately he pressed himself against the railing of the bridge. The car charged past him with only an inch or two to spare.

Then the car shifted into reverse and came rushing backwards. It skidded to a stop right next to Damien. Randall leaped out, a knife glittering in his hand.

Again Damien's eyes made a frantic sweep around. There was no one else near the bridge. And the chances of somebody seeing him from below and stopping to help were slim.

Randall slowly stalked towards Damien.

"Come on, Randall," said Damien fearfully. "You're already in enough trouble for stealing. What'll happen if you kill somebody? You'll be running for the rest of your life."

Randall bared his teeth. "I don't think so, little man," he hissed. "I've killed a couple people in my time. None of 'em ever got up to complain about it afterwards."

Randall inched closer. Damien couldn't take his eyes off the knife. It glittered like ice, almost hypnotizing him.

"Ever hear about the first one I killed?" continued Randall. "It was the day I'd stolen my first Caddie. I drove that baby around half the city. And I'm not just talking roads." Randall's laughter was a hateful bark. "Sidewalks too. You shoulda seen people jumpin' outta my way!"

Randall's smile became huge and vicious. "One fool didn't have the sense to jump fast enough," he said. "He was crossing the street. You know what that fool did? Walked right into my car. Dented the bumper and everything. Maybe you 'member him?"

Damien went numb with shock. "You—you ran down my dad?"

Randall laughed. "You know, you're as

big a fool as your daddy. Say hello to him
for me, little man.''

Quick as a cat, Randall lunged at
Damien. Without stopping to think,
Damien kicked Randall in the knee as
hard as he could. To Damien's surprise,
the kick dislodged the knife from Randall's hand. The blade rattled across the
pavement as Randall clutched his knee.

Damien made a desperate leap for the
knife. He hoped to grab it and throw it
as far away as he could. But Randall
lunged again. Savagely he slammed into
Damien's ankle. Then wrapping his hands
around Damien's neck, he pinned Damien
against the railing.

Though his ankle was screaming in
pain, Damien fought wildly. But
Randall's grip was like a band of concrete.

Damien could see the cars and trucks
flowing by far below. Inch by inch,
Randall was forcing him over the rail.

''See those cars?'' Randall panted.
''Don't look so big from up here, huh? But
down below . . . Which do you figure is going to finish you off? The fall? Or the front

end of some semi?''

Damien kept struggling, but it was hopeless. One more push, and he'd be over the edge.

Dimly, Damien heard the sound of a car coming to a stop nearby. Then in an instant, Damien felt Randall's body jerk backwards. Damien and Randall lurched away from the railing. Damien tumbled from Randall's loosened grip.

Damien looked up to see Willis Tate struggling with Randall. Will's black sedan stood by, its motor still running.

"Will!" Damien gasped.

Randall wrenched himself away from Will. Scooping up the knife, he turned back to Will and started to move in.

Will and Randall circled each other. The two men were about the same height and weight. But Randall was young and tough. Will's many hard years had taken their toll on his strength.

Suddenly Will lunged forward and tried to grab the knife. Randall swiftly dodged back. Then he lashed out with the knife, grazing Will's face. A streak of blood appeared.

Damien tried to stand up and nearly yelled from the pain in his leg. Yet he managed to throw himself forward and grab Randall's leg.

Randall quickly shoved Damien to the side. But for a second, he was off balance. And in that second, Will leaped forward and grabbed the knife.

Suddenly Randall and Will were locked together, struggling over the knife. The two of them spun toward the railing. Will's back slammed so hard against it that he gasped for air. The knife clattered over the side of the bridge.

Now Will was in the same position Damien had been in. Randall's steely hands fixed around Will's neck. Slowly but surely, the younger man was pushing Will over the rail.

With a wild cry, Damien tried to go to Will's aid. He fell twice before managing to stand up.

As Damien hobbled forward, he noticed a strange expression on Will's face. Will was inches away from death. Yet he looked completely calm. His blue eyes told Damien that he didn't feel a trace of fear.

At last Damien got close enough to grab hold of Randall's belt. He gave Randall a furious tug. Randall swung around and lashed Damien to the ground. Then with renewed fury, he threw himself upon Will again.

But this time, Will's grip proved stronger. He hung tight to the railing. And Randall's own weight carried him over the edge.

Damien didn't see Randall strike the freeway below. He just saw that Randall was gone. And Will was still alive.

Damien suddenly began to sob with relief. He shook and cried as though he'd never stop.

Gently Will bent down beside Damien and held him. For several minutes, they stayed like that.

Finally Damien felt the horror and panic fade a little. He drew back and gazed at Will. He now saw that Will's hand as well as his cheek were badly cut.

"You're hurt," Damien managed to

stammer.

"I'll be all right," said Will.

"Will, you—you saved my life," said Damien. "You risked getting killed for me."

Will shook his head. "Don't try to make me into a hero, Damien. I've just been keeping an eye out for you."

Damien gave a shaky laugh. "Now who's being too shy?"

Will only smiled and helped Damien to the car.

In a few minutes, the police arrived. It turned out that a few people on the freeway had seen the fight. They all agreed that Will had acted in self-defense.

Shortly afterwards, an ambulance pulled up. Randall's body was loaded onto a stretcher and covered with a sheet. Then the ambulance drove slowly away. There was no siren. There was no need for one now.

After getting statements, the police escorted Will and Damien to the hospital. Will's cuts required some stitches. And the doctor wrapped Damien's sprained ankle.

Damien's mother met them at the hospital. When she saw Damien, she clutched him in a hug so tight, it left him breathless. Then she turned to Will.

"Thank God you were there, Will," she said quietly. Willis Tate quietly nodded.

Will drove the three of them home to the Blairs' apartment. With Will on one side and his mother on the other, Damien made it up the stairs without too much trouble.

Once the three were inside the apartment, Will turned to go. "Wait, Will," his mother called. She hesitated for a moment. Then she suggested, "Won't you stay and at least have something to drink?"

Damien saw a look pass between them. Will apparently read her gaze and slowly nodded.

As they sat around the table, Damien's mother cleared her throat. "Did you ever tell Damien, Will?" she asked softly.

Will lowered his head slightly. "I wanted to," he said. "But I was planning to talk with you first."

Damien felt strange. Somehow, he knew that his life was going to change in the next few moments. He knew that things would never be the same again. But he didn't know why or how.

Damien's mother gazed at Will. She seemed to be waiting for him to speak. But Will remained silent.

"What is it?" asked Damien breathlessly.

His mother turned and looked at him. "Damien, the night you were born, Charles Blair was with me. He loved you and he took care of you for three years. In my mind and in his, he was your real father. No father could have loved his son more.

"But, honey, Charles wasn't your biological father. Will is."

"Will?" Damien exclaimed. He sat back and stared at Willis Tate. It was the most amazing news he'd ever heard.

Even so, he didn't exactly feel surprised. A thousand mysteries suddenly seemed to have been solved. And Damien felt that a part of him had known this secret all along.

His mother leaned forward and took his hand. "Damien, Will and I fell in love. He even asked me to marry him. And I agreed.

"But as time passed, I saw we'd made a terrible mistake. Will's drinking problem really got out of hand. I figured that any man who drank like that couldn't really be happy with me."

"Jessie, please," Will protested. "You know I started drinking long before I met you. You had nothing to do with turning me into an alcoholic. I did that all by myself."

Damien's mother gazed steadily into Will's eyes. "Thank you for that, Will."

Then his mother sighed and sat back. "Well, we separated. And I went back to my childhood sweetheart—Charles."

"Did he know . . . I mean . . . " Words failed Damien.

"If you mean did he know I was pregnant with Will's child, the answer is yes."

His mother looked down at her clasped

hands. It struck Damien that she must be staring at the simple wedding ring Charles Blair had given her all those years ago.

Then she raised her head. "When you were born, I wrote Will a letter about you. And I sent pictures. I kept sending him news over the years."

"But I never came to see you, Damien," said Will shamefacedly. "I was either drunk or in jail. But about three years ago, I quit drinking. I finally started getting my life together. This year I wrote Jessie and asked her if I could come and see you."

Damien's mother nodded. "At first, I was scared witless when Will said he wanted to see you. But then I saw it was his right. And yours, Damien."

So that was why his mother had been shaken by the news of Damien's "shadow man." His mother had suspected all along that it was Willis Tate.

Damien turned and stared at Will. "So you're my real father," he managed to say at last.

"No," Willis Tate said. "Charles Blair loved you even before you were born. He's your father. But I'd like to be your friend."

Then before Damien could answer, Will got up. "See you later, Damien. Jessie."

Damien heard the question in Will's voice. It was a question he didn't feel prepared to answer just yet.

\* \* \*

Brad Stanton was caught by the police the next day. He confessed to the robbery and to threatening Damien. He even admitted writing Damien the first note. But he maintained that Randall had broken into Damien's locker and left the second note. Later, Damien heard that Brad had been sent to a juvenile home.

Damien felt no emotion at the news. Nor did he feel anything when Randall Jones was buried—only a kind of sad relief. Randall would never hurt anyone again.

Meanwhile, Mr. Hall's play went on as

planned. Damien kept his part as Sydney Carton, though he limped around awkwardly on stage.

At the end, Damien stood by the fake guillotine that James had built. He couldn't help shaking a little when he spoke Sydney Carton's last words. He remembered the calm expression on Will's face just before Randall had died. At the most dangerous moment of his life, Will had felt no fear.

So there really are some Sydney Cartons around, Damien thought. As if they agreed with that thought, the audience broke into applause. The play was over, and Damien took his bows.

\* \* \*

In the weeks that followed, Ben Winters started coming to dinner every Sunday night. Ben turned out to be good company. He told wild stories that made Damien laugh. And he asked for and listened to Damien's opinions.

Damien decided that he liked Ben more

with every visit. And he noticed his mother seemed to feel the same way too.

As much as Damien enjoyed Ben's company, he looked forward to seeing Will even more. Whenever the black car pulled up in front of the apartment, Damien would race down to meet it. He felt a little shy at first. But he and Will grew more comfortable together.

One day when they were tossing around a football in the park, Damien looked at Will's face.

"You know, your scar has almost healed," said Damien.

"Yeah," said Will.

"Nobody will even be able to see it before too long."

"Maybe not," said Will. "Most ugly things do fade after a while."

Damien nodded. He knew that Will was talking about much more than a scar.

"Hey, I've got a couple of tickets to the football game tomorrow," Will announced.

"All right! So—who're you going with?" he prodded.

"Who do you think?" said Will.

Damien smiled broadly. And as soon as he got home, he asked his mother if he could go. "Fine with me," she said. "But only if you promise not to give me a play-by-play afterwards," she added with a grin.

The game the next day was fantastic. The home team scored the winning touchdown in the last twenty seconds. Damien nearly yelled himself hoarse.

On the drive home, Damien and Will discussed the game for a while. Then they both fell silent, mulling over their own thoughts.

Finally Damien turned to Will. "You know, I keep forgetting you're my father," he said.

"It's probably best that way," Will replied. "Charles was there when you needed him. He's your father."

Damien studied Will. He saw a worn but honest, warm face. Damien thought it was a good face. But right now, Will's blue eyes looked sad.

Damien hesitated. Then he said, "I was

real little when my dad died. To me, he's always been this young guy in a high school graduation picture."

Will nodded understandingly.

"What I'm saying is, I never really had a dad to give me advice. Oh, Mama's great. But sometimes I just wish there was some older guy to tell me . . . well, to tell me if I'm completely crazy or only a little."

Will chuckled softly. "You got my blood in you, Damien. Bound to be 'completely.' "

Damien laughed too. "So how about it, Will? You sticking around?"

He tried to keep the question casual. Yet so much rode on Will's answer.

"I'd like to," Will replied. "In fact, now that I know I'm welcome, I'd like that a lot."

Damien smiled and leaned back into the warm sun. If the day had started with any shadows, they were now just a memory.